PROJECT: HERO

By Rick L. Phillips

PREVIOUS BOOKS BY THE AUTHOR

DINKY THE ELF
IT'S THAT TIME AGAIN VOLUME 3 (SHORT STORY TITLED
"WAR BETWEEN TWO WORLDS")
LAST TRAIN TO MURDER
WITH GREAT POWER

AUTHORS BLOG
HTTP://THEOFFICIALBLOGOFRICKLPHILLIPSAUTHOR.BLOGSPOT.COM

COVER ART BY
DAVID C MOREFIELD
HTTP://SUPERMANFAN.NU/NIGHTWING

ISBN-13: 978-0692300831
ISBN-10: 069230083X

THIS BOOK IS DEDICATED TO MY LORD AND SAVIOUR
JESUS CHRIST, TO MY WIFE VIOLET FOR HER LOVE AND
SUPPORT AND TO MY MOM AND DAD WHO LED ME TO
CHRIST AND GAVE ME COMIC BOOKS TO HELP ME TO
LEARN TO READ.

Chapter 1

Origin Story

Daniel Urich is a man of enormous wealth. He is a multi-billionaire thanks to an inheritance from his Uncle, Bill Urich. He ran a weapons manufacturing business with contracts to the government. Early on Daniel liquidated that business and used the money to fund his Urich Foundation. He now gives money back to those in need of his assistance. He has a mansion in an exclusive gated community. How exclusive? He bought the whole community. He is the sole resident with the exception of his right-hand man Louis. Mr. Urich is at all of the big events in town and constantly has a woman on his arm. He is a man of principals and conviction but he also loves the limelight and it loves him back. He is in his early 50's and seems to have it all.

Still his life has not been without tragedy. At the age of 9 he lost his parents in a car accident. The only living relative was his Father's brother Bill. He took the boy in and raised him as if he were his own son. Eventually, Daniel put his parent's death in the back of his mind. He was happy and well adjusted. He was the Captain of the football team and had a steady girlfriend. Then when he was 18 and near the end of his senior year in high school his Uncle Bill died of a heart attack. At least it looked that way at first. After an autopsy, they found a poison in his blood that really killed him. The police did their best and even Daniel was a suspect for a time. There was no evidence to link anyone to the death of Bill Urich and the case remains unsolved to this day.

Daniel became distant. He hardly talked to anyone and pushed his girlfriend away. He graduated high school and was happy to see his Uncle's butler Louis at the ceremony but wished that his Uncle and his parents could be there too. He went to college for a few months as a chemistry major but dropped out. Louis was disappointed and told him that his Uncle would be too. Daniel said he could learn more about life if he just traveled the world and took off to parts unknown. He did keep in touch with Louis by letters for awhile then stopped writing. When he was 21 he came into his full inheritance. He didn't come back on his own. No one knew where he was and if Louis hadn't hired a detective to track him down the whole estate would have gone to the Government and they would have sold everything and put everyone out of work.

Everyone expected that Daniel would just appoint someone to run the business for him. Instead, he took over and to everyone's surprise he took to it very well. Some say he ran it better than his Uncle. Daniel didn't like making weapons that hurt people and once the current contracts were filled he changed the business into the current foundation. While he is wealthy, his wealth has grown very little as every profit he makes is funneled back into the foundation and a special project that only he and Louis know about. You see Daniel is, or rather was, the superhero known as the Terror. Not only was his Uncle murdered but he suspects his parents were too. His Father was a police detective and Daniel has always felt that the car accident wasn't really an accident. He loved living the life of a playboy and helping the less fortunate with his foundation, but his real passion was fighting crime and to find the real killers of his family.

He has recently retired from crime fighting, at least in the physical sense. He still keeps up to date on the news and helps the police when he can and still investigates his family's deaths. But he couldn't keep up with the battles. Louis himself is still around too. He should have retired long ago but stays on to help Daniel.

Today another tragedy has entered the life of Daniel Urich. When he turned on the early morning news he heard of a homeless man who was in his early 90's whose name was Ross Martin who was found dead from a heart attack. He was lying in the gutter in a side street. Normally this would not be newsworthy on what was a busy news day and even Daniel would not know him by that name. But the reporter said that police traced his fingerprints to reveal that Mr. Martin was the World War II superhero Flag-waver. As he falls back into his chair Louis comes into the room.

"What is it sir? You look distressed."
"Flag-waver is dead."

Louis is as stunned as Daniel, but his practice of keeping a straight face holds true to form. The only thing that gives away any clue to his emotion is when he stands closer to Daniel and places a comforting hand on his shoulder.

Daniel gets up. He strolls over to look out his penthouse window. He clasps his hands behind his back as he stares blankly out the window at that vast expanse of the city below him.

"He was a good man. He was already a legend when I met him. I was 21 years old and had just begun my own private war on crime as the Terror."

He walks over to his desk. He presses a button and a secret drawer pops open. Out of that drawer, he pulls out two photographs. Both have Flag-waver pictured with another man in different costumes. He shows one to Louis.

"This one has Flag-waver in that red, white and blue costume that he always wore. I am of course in that gaudy rainbow costume next to him. I didn't have much fashion sense as a superhero. Going by my comic book collection I thought all superheroes wore bright colors."

"What made you change it?"
He shows the second picture to Louis. The stances of the two men are almost identical from the first picture, but the Terror is now in an all

black costume.

"Flag told me he wore a bright colored costume of red, white and blue because he represented America during World War II. Other heroes had superpowers and if they brought attention to themselves they had the power to defend themselves. But a non-powered person like myself needed the element of surprise. I should be more of a creature of the night and blend into the darkness."

"I knew back then that you were fighting crime," said Louis. "I couldn't stop you as you were an adult and not a child. I didn't know that you were part of a team."

"I really wasn't. We teamed-up on some cases, but we weren't a team. His partner, Kid Patriot, quit crime fighting years before and he ask me to take his place. My war on crime was not something that was done because I was a patriot. Mine was a private war of revenge. I didn't want to drag him into it. From the times I was with him I did learn a lot."

"How much time passed between these photos?"

"Maybe two years. Why?"

"You were 21 then. Yet it looks like Flag-waver

was still in his twenties as well. In the second photo, you haven't changed much but Flag-waver looks to have more wrinkles. It's a bit hard to tell much more with the costumes covering almost all of you, but I would say he looks like he has aged 10 years during those two years."

"I noticed that back then too. I guess time was just catching up with him."

"He isn't wearing a belt in the second picture."

"Yeah, he told me the first time that he lost it and was trying to find it. Next time I saw him I noticed that he still didn't have the belt. He made a joke of it. He said as long as his pants didn't fall down while in a fight he didn't need it."

Daniel is smiling at that last thought as he puts the picture down and sits behind his desk. His smile quickly changes into a serious look. He picks up the picture again. He stares at it intently.

"It isn't fair."

"What isn't fair sir?"

"There are other heroes out there like Flag. They think of fighting crime as a public service. They don't have a job they just rely on any reward that they get for stopping the crime. Others do have a job but since they keep their identity secret they always run the risk of losing their job every time they rush off to stop a crime."

"I suppose most of them aren't as fortunate as you to have a fortune to rely on."

"Something needs to be done about that."

"I suppose you think you are the one to do that sir."

"I am someone in a position to do that."

"How?"

"Maybe I could get the word out that the heroes have a friend in the Urich Foundation. We could hire them and pay them well to work low-level jobs. That way they stay under the radar and won't be missed if they are out fighting crime."

"How do you intend to do that?"

"Give me some time to think about it. I don't want any more patriots dying penniless in the gutters."

Chapter 2

The Master Plan

A few days later Louis is waxing the limo in the Urich mansion's garage when the intercom comes on. The voice of Daniel Urich can be heard loud and clear.

"Louis, could you please come into the study. I need you."

Louis stops waxing and without a word he leaves the garage. He walks through the vast mansion and passes huge rooms that its owner rarely, if ever, uses. Moments later he opens the huge double doors to the study. At the end of the study sits Daniel Urich behind his oak desk. Louis' footsteps click on the marble floor as he walks the length of the room. He stands in front of the desk. Daniel looks up.

"Don't be so formal Louis. Sit down."

He sits in an overstuffed chair in front of the desk.

"I presume you have called me in to discuss your project hero."

"Yes our business of Champions. I don't think it will be too hard to put them on the payroll with their real names. Any additional expense we can put under miscellaneous expenses."

"But how will you let the news out to the superhero community?"

"It may require me putting on the Terror costume again."

"Surely you won't be going into battle at your age?"

"Not if I don't have to. Mainly all I want to do is get in touch with Police Chief O'Bryan."

"He never had a great love for you as the Terror. He always thought you were the criminal kingpin of the city."

"I know but he always recognized the value that the superhero community offered to the city. In a few years, he will be eligible for retirement. He may be the last trustworthy cop on the force. If we have no heroes left because of financial concerns then what will happen to our good citizens."

"So your business of champions is needed."

"I believe everything happens for a reason. I regret that it took Flag-Wavers death, but it did get my attention to getting this started."

That night Chief O'Bryan leaves the Police Station he gets in his car and pulls away. Suddenly He hears a familiar voice from the backseat.

"It's good to see you again O'Bryan."

The hairs on the back of his neck stand on end. This is a voice he hadn't heard in years and had hoped to never hear again. His eyes dart quickly to his rear view mirror. Once again, he only sees darkness but out of that darkness looking back at him is the steely gaze of... the Terror.

"What an unpleasant surprise," says O'Bryan. "I haven't heard from you for so long I started to believe the rumors that you had retired."

"I did. I had to come out of retirement to pass a message to you."

"What's the message? You want me to stop hassling one of your goons?"

"You've always believed I played both ends. Well, maybe this will convince you I don't. The Urich Foundation has started a new top secret project. Daniel Urich knows that some superheroes have a hard time paying the bills. Flag-waver, dying homeless proved this to him and the world. Daniel Urich got in touch with me telling me that he will secretly hire them to do menial work. He'll give them time to offer their services to the community like they always have. Mr. Urich wants you to give any heroes in that position this card. He calls it Project: Hero."

The Terror puts his gloved hand over the front seat. In his hand is a thick stack of cards. O'Bryan stops at a red traffic light. He takes the cards from the Terror.

"Normally I would say this is baloney Terror but if Daniel Urich is involved it may be on the level. I know Urich personally. I'll be contacting him to make sure you're telling the truth."

O'Bryan waits for the Terror to say something. All he hears is silence.

"Did you hear me Terror?" He turns to look in the backseat and sees it is empty. He never even heard the back door open or close.

"I hate it when he does that."

Chapter 3

A Visit From The Chief

The next day Daniel Urich gets an expected visitor at the Urich Foundation as the secretary buzzes him in.

"Chief O'Bryan," says Daniel as he comes from behind his desk. He extends his hand in greeting. "To what do I owe the pleasure of this visit?"

The Chief shakes Daniel's hand.

"This isn't a friendly visit. Do you know that a mask vigilante is giving out one of your addresses?"

Daniel goes back to his desk. He takes his seat and presses a button.

"Miss Johnson! Please hold all calls and any visitors till the Chief and I are done."

"Yes Mr. Urich," she replies.

"Well?" Ask the Chief.

"Yes I know about it."

"How can you let a suspected criminal have your address?"

"You and I have both worked with the Terror on many occasions. While you have always suspected he was a criminal it has never been proven."

"I admit that he has always helped us, but it was by getting inside information," says the Chief.

"Yes but that is because they always believed he was a criminal mastermind. I'm sure he was undercover."

"I always thought he was just leading us to the smaller jobs and he had others take care of the big ones while we were distracted. "

"What bigger jobs? When the President was visiting the foundation it was the Terror who told us how the Stooge was going to kidnap him. He only got that info because one of the Stooge's henchmen trusted him."

"Yes and it was the Stooge who ordered that man killed while he was still in jail."

Daniel's face turns sad as he recalls the moment that he heard that news.

"That was a regrettable after effect of the operation."

"My point is maybe the Terror wanted that man dead and he used the Stooge to do it."

"Why would he want that man dead?"

"I don't know."

"What you do know is that the Stooge was found to have given that order. After a fair trial, the Stooge now has life in prison. He won't bother society again and you have the Terror to thank for it."

The Chief walks away to leave. He put his hand on the door knob. He opens the door. We see another man in the outer office waiting. He rises halfway but then the Chief closes the door. He turns and looks back at Daniel.

"What about Fly Man?"

"What about him?"

"He made flying bombs that he flew into buildings so they would explode. Usually, it has been to cover up another crime he was doing."

"I don't remember him having any tussles' with the Terror. He seemed to always fight the Golden Guardian."

"Yes but it was always when the Terror was never around."

"You're not suggesting…"

"Yes! He told Fly Man when he wouldn't be in town and that let him go on a killing spree. At least he would have if not for the Guardian. May he rest in peace."

"I know he was Fly Man's last victim."

"Not intended. He was killed in a fight when one of those bombs exploded in his face. That bomb was meant for me. He saved my life and if the Terror had something to do with it I want him arrested."

"For goodness sakes O'Bryan the Terror can't always be around. He can't be everywhere."

"I guess not. Come to think of it most of those times you weren't in town either."

Daniel gets nervous. He tugs at his collar.

"Well, I… eh… can't be in town all the time either O'Bryan. I… do have a worldwide foundation to run as you well know. Besides you still can't prove that the Terror had anything to do with that. Fly Man is still on the loose. I suggest that you concentrate on finding him."

"Well, how about the Flapper?"

"You mean that girl who thinks it's still the 1920's?"

"Yes. It's no secret that she was attracted to the Terror."

"Well, you and the Terror always stopped her crimes."

"Yes but she always got away. Maybe she was the Terror's girlfriend and he let her get away. No matter how good a man the Terror is that is a felony."

Daniel rubs his brow and lowers his head for a moment. Then he looks back up.

"An interesting theory but again you still don't have any proof. Can't you just take the Terror at face value like I have?"

"I just have a hard time believing that a man who dresses in all black and wears a mask is on the side of the Angels."

"Just because a man wears black doesn't mean he is a bad guy. Just like a person who wears white isn't always the good guy."

"Name me one crook who wears white. They always wear dark colors so they can hide from the law. That's why most crimes are committed at night." Says O'Bryan.

"There's the Albino Lion. There's Madame White Snake who is jailed in China. There's White Noise the burglar who makes alarms go silent. There's..."

"I only said name one."

The Chief stands motionless by the door looking a little annoyed. Daniel gives a slight smile as he knows the Chief is beginning to see his point.

"Chief, if you don't trust the Terror, do you at least trust me and my judgment?"

"I do."

"Then why are we arguing about this?"

"Because I wanted to make sure you were thinking clearly and not taken in by a crook. Now I know that you are thinking clearly."

"Then you will pass on the address to any who need it?"

"I will."

The Chief turns to the door. He turns the doorknob but before he pulls it open he looks back towards Daniel.

"I doubt I'll see the Terror again anytime soon. So tell him I said hello if you see him when you're doing business out of town."

He then opens the door and leaves. Daniel slumps in his chair and wonders how this will all turn out.

Chapter 4

Membership Drive

It is a few weeks later. At 1 AM, the police have an abandoned warehouse surrounded. There is a burglar that has taken refuge there. He broke into a family's home only to rob them but an old woman surprised him and he accidentally shot her. She died instantly. Out of blind panic he ran. He found this warehouse and hid. It only bought him a few hours. Even a four-year-old could have followed the trail that he unknowingly left. But the street the warehouse is on was a dead-end and it was the last building on the street. Thanks to a thunderstorm, the evening was even darker than normal with only moments of illumination from the lightening. Chief O'Bryan is barking orders to his men as the rain comes down in buckets.

"Get those searchlights up! Get some snipers on that roof across the street!"

"Chief!"

"What is it officer?"

"Shouldn't we call in a hostage negotiator?"

"There are no hostages."

"Then why don't we just storm in and take him?"

"It's because that is a very old building. Even with a blueprint I don't trust going in there. I want that scum caught, but I need to keep my men safe. Now get back to your position."

The officer leaves. Just then, there is a flash of lightening and out of the corner of his eye O'Bryan sees something. It looked like an arch that stretched from rooftop to rooftop and then disappeared. He calls to the officer again.

"Officer!"

He stops on his way back to his position. He turns to face the chief.

"Yes sir!"

"Did you see that?"

"See what?"

"Up on the roof."

"The snipers? Yes they just got up there."

"I guess that is what it was. Get to your position."

The officer turns and starts on his way back. Suddenly there is a noise coming from the inside the warehouse. O'Bryan wonders what is going on. He radios the Detective in charge.

"I didn't give the order for you to move in."

"I know. We haven't sent anyone in yet."

O'Bryan wonders what is making the noise from inside. Suddenly he doesn't hear anything at all from the warehouse. Just then, the burglar is lowered in front of O'Bryan on what looks like an orange rope. O'Bryan looks up to see stretching down from the rooftops is the city's newest superhero Mr. Stretchable and the orange rope is really his arm wrapped around the crook.

"Burglar/murderer caught and delivered Police Chief O'Bryan." Says Mr. Stretchable.

"Thanks. With a new superhero popping up every day, I wonder why the city needs the police."

"Well, we can't be everywhere Chief. Somebody has to catch the jaywalkers."

O'Bryan looks at him with disgust.

"We'll take care of him from here Stretchable."

"Actually Chief I was hoping there may be a reward. Money is a little tight right now."

O'Bryan remembers his promise to Daniel.

"Look if you need money take this card."

He hands him Daniel's business card.

"How is this going to help?"

"Just go to that address. I've given it to others that are in the same situation as you. I'm sure someone will explain it there."

Mr. Stretchable gives his thanks. He stretches to the height of the warehouse and steps over it. Quickly Chief O'Bryan heads to his squad car. Instead of grabbing his radio to call headquarters he takes out his cell phone and quickly dials Daniel.

Soon Mr. Stretchable reaches his destination. He regains his normal height and looks over the area. The block is a vacant lot surrounded by rundown buildings. Near one of the buildings is an old phone booth. He hears the phone ringing.

"You hardly ever see one of those anymore." He thinks to himself. "Especially one that still works."

He goes over to the booth. Opens the sliding glass door and enters. He picks up the receiver. Then he hears a voice on the other end.

"Hang up the phone."

"Why?" He ask out of habit. But they have already hung up.

He hangs up the receiver. As soon as he does the bottom of the phone booth quickly lowers. When it stops he is three stories below the street. A door slides open and Mr. Stretchable steps out. There is a long hallway that he walks down. His footsteps echo with each step. He sees a door at the far end.

"Someone has watched way too many reruns of Get Smart." He says out loud. He hears the echo of his voice come back to him.

Finally, he reaches the end of the hall. He places his hand on the doorknob.

"I wonder if I'll find Don Adams or Barbara Feldon on the other side?" He thinks to himself.

He turns the knob and opens the door. As he steps into the room it lights up. In the center of the room, he sees Daniel Urich. He is surrounded by colorfully clad individuals. Daniel steps forward.

"Welcome to the Urich Foundation's Project: Hero Mr. Stretchable! I am Daniel Urich."

"Definitely not Don Adams."

"Come again?"

"Never mind! How can you and your people here help me with my finances?"

"O'Bryan phoned us and vouched for you. I have started a new project at the foundation called Project: Hero."

A man wearing only swim trunks steps forward.

"He is willing to pay us well to do menial tasks and look the other way when we are absent solving crimes."

Mr. Stretchable looks at the man and then his face lights up with recognition.

"I know you. Aren't you called Sea King?"

"Yes," he says with a resignation in his voice that gives away that he doesn't really like that name.

"If you're the King of Atlantis why are you going to work as a paper pusher?"

"I'm not the King of Atlantis. That was something a reporter dreamed up to sell more newspapers when I first appeared. No matter how many times I say it's not true people seem to want to believe I am King of Atlantis. But I am only a citizen who was exiled from Atlantis. Being half an air breather, I am not allowed to live there."

"But you still protect Atlantis."

"I protect all people whether they like me or not."

Daniel looks at Mr. Stretchable. Then he turns toward a blue-skinned man standing in the corner.

"Perhaps the rest of the recruits should tell you the rest of the story. Venusian Visionary would you like to add more of the information?"

"We do have to supply Mr. Urich with our alter ego in order to get paid. I could add more, but I think it best to leave the rest to the others."

Suddenly a voice from nowhere is heard.

"Mr. Urich said he understands if we still want to keep our real names private."

"Who said that?"

A shimmering light leaps off of Daniel Urich's shoulder. It grows bigger as it hits the ground. The colors of red and yellow flash brighter as it gets bigger. Suddenly it takes the image of a 5'9" tall man in a red and yellow costume.

"I said that. May I introduce myself? I am the Atomic Sprite."

"Ofcourseheisaverytrustwrothymansowecantrusthimwithourrealnames."

"Hey, slow down fellow. You're running your words together. Are you even standing still? All I see is a green blur."

The green blur slows down to reveal the green and yellow image of another man.

"Sorry, I am so used to doing everything fast that I forget I need to slow down sometimes. I'm called Accelerate. I was saying that Mr. Urich is very trustworthy so we can trust him with our real names."

Suddenly there is a rush of wind through the air. Mr. Stretchable quickly bends out of the way. Accelerate quickly grabs the weapon before it can strike the wall. The weapon is a bolo. A female figure garbed in a dark brown hooded costume and wearing a brown mask around her eyes steps from the shadows.

"That was just to test your reaction time. It was quite impressive."

"Thanks and just who are you?"

"People call me the Brown Bolo."

Suddenly a door opens from the back of the room. A huge man dressed in gold steps forward. He extends his arm straight out. He bends his fist down and a beam shoots forward from a wristband on his arm. The beam forms a golden globe around Mr. Stretchable. From inside the globe, we hear him speak.

"Hey, what gives?"

He tries every form but cannot find a way out of the globe. Suddenly he takes the shape of a ball. He grows bigger and bigger. The man in the gold outfit starts to show the signs of strain on his face. Beads of sweat form on his forehead. Suddenly the ball is too big and the golden globe pops. Mr. Stretchable reforms in midair to his human self and floats to the floor. Mr. Urich smiles as he steps between the two.

"It looks like it's going to be a duel between who our most powerful member will be. Mr. Stretchable meet the Golden Guardian."

The two men shake hands.

"I thought you were dead. But here you are and you look younger than I thought."

"That was my Father. I have decided to continue with the family business."

"Oh! Well, that's great you continue to fight crime but I am sorry for your loss."

"Thank you but he went the way he wanted, serving mankind."

Daniel is all smiles as he looks at them all.

"People I believe this is the beginning of a great adventure for all of us."

Chapter 5

The Mysterious Call

The following weeks pass quickly. The project is running smoothly. Crime still happens and some of the heroes do have to take some time off. Mr. Stretchable took off to track down the villain Putty Puss. Brown Bolo took off time to take down Professor Menace. Still the biggest news came in when Atomic Sprite had to team-up with Venusian Visionary to take on someone who seemed to be a harmless businessman named Zachary Zimmerman. He was really running a worldwide criminal empire from a small store on Main Street and was setting up to take over the world till they stopped him. Yet with all this, their greatest adventure still lay ahead. It all started when Daniel Urich got an unexpected phone call.

It was 2AM at Urich Mansion. Daniel hears a knock on his bedroom door. He gets wearily out of bed. He goes to his closet and gets his robe and puts it on. He wobbles sleepily to the door and opens it. There stands Louis in his nightshirt and slippers. Daniel gives him an angry look.

"Well, what is it?"

"Sorry to bother you sir but there is an urgent phone call for you."

"It better be urgent. I had a long day and was welcoming staying home in bed all night."
"I think when you hear who is on the other end you may want to change your plans."

"Who is it?"

"You better take the call."

Louis smiles and turns to go back to his bed. As he wobbles down the long hallway Daniel closes the door. It wasn't a slam but the door is so heavy that its sound echoes through the house. Slightly more awake Daniel walks a little bit straighter as he heads toward his phone. He unplugged it before bed to sleep uninterrupted, but that didn't work out. He plugs it back in and picks up the receiver. He takes the call but hears Louis waiting on the other end.

"You can hang up the phone Louis I have the call. This is Daniel Urich. To whom am I speaking? "

Daniel's face goes pale when he hears the name. It's a name he heard years ago but didn't think he would ever hear it again. A full minute passes as he listens to the voice on the other end. When he does speak it is just one short sentence.

"Yes I'll meet you there."

A few minutes later a fully dressed Daniel passes Louis in the hallway. He is still in his nightshirt and slippers. He hasn't made it back to bed yet.

"Going out Mr. Urich?"

"I have to meet with an old friend. Mind the manor for me will you please Louis?"

"As always sir."

Louis gets Daniel his coat and helps him put it on. He thanks, Louis and heads for the car. Louis gets ready to change, but Daniel calls back to him.

"You don't have to drive me Louis. I'll drive myself."

With that he gets in the car and drives down the long winding driveway till he is out of sight.

Twenty minutes later he is waiting in his office at the Urich Foundation. The place is empty. Still he hears a knock at his office door.

"The doors unlocked you can come in."

The door slowly opens. On the other side is a man who is somewhere in his late 80's. As he walks across the vast expanse of the office his footsteps click on the floor. Finally, he stops in front of Daniel's desk. Daniel is seated and motions for the man to take a seat.

As he sat there Daniel could only stare at him. He only saw the man once but was amazed at how well he had held up over the years.

"It's been a long time George." Says Daniel.

"Over 30 years since the only time we met. I'm surprised that you still remember me."

"You don't forget when you meet a living legend like Kid Patriot."

"No one's called me that name in years." Says George.

"You've been retired since then and I heard that even Flag-waver rarely heard from you."

"We did meet from time to time. That is how I know what I am about to tell you."

"So what is important enough that it would bring you out of hiding?"

"I wasn't hiding. Anyone could have found me. Most people just didn't look."

"Still what was important enough that it couldn't wait a few more hours?"
"You remember the colors of Flag-wavers

costume?"

"Of course! It was very patriotic. Red, white and blue."

"Yes but there was one part that was gold. It was his belt."

"I know he quit wearing it after a while."

Daniel knew it was more than that but wanted to see if George knew.

"He didn't just quit. He lost it."

"There were rumors that he got his powers from that belt. I never believed it. How could a belt give someone powers?"

"You should have believed it because it was true. It not only gave him his super strength or his invulnerability, but there was another power that most didn't know about."

"What was it?"

"Eternal youth."

"The man died of old age. How did he have eternal youth?"

"He had it till the belt went missing. When you and I first met, Flag and I would talk, when you weren't around, about the belt. He wore it so long that his powers became part of him, but they were slowly fading. As a result, he started aging and his strength became less and less super. He was always looking for the belt. He suspected that it was in the wrong hands and was being experimented with. They just haven't found out how to work it yet."

"How does it work?"

"Ross said it would only work for him. I don't know how Ross figured that out."

"George, if it only worked for Ross why worry? They won't be able to use it."

"That's what I always told him."

"So there isn't anything to worry about."

"Ross was worried for years about where that belt was. He always said it would only work for him but after it went missing he started questioning himself."

"What questions did he ask himself?"

"He wondered if it would only work with a

certain body chemistry or mentality."

"If someone found it they must not have the same chemistry. Otherwise, we would have heard from them by now."

"What if they are trying to find the one who has that body chemistry? We could be in for a rough time in the future."

Daniel strokes his chin thoughtfully. He leans back and looks at George.

"So why are you telling me all this? Why not tell an active superhero or even the Police?"

"The Police would just think I was a crazy old man and I've been out of the hero business a long time so I don't know the new heroes and the others are either dead or in too bad a shape to do anything. I'm not much better myself, but I thought with you, we could find it together. Also, with your money you may have resources I don't."

Daniel straightens up and leans forward on his desk. He looks George square in the eyes.

"I have resources that you wouldn't believe."

Chapter 6

The Living Legend

Later that night Daniel meets again with his friend George Kirby in a basement library of the foundation. The room is sparsely furnished. It is lined with bookcases filled with books. There are only two tables in the room and there are four wooden chairs at each table, other than that there is nothing in the room.

"I guess we should have some privacy down here." Says George.

"It's about to get even more private." Replies Daniel.

Without another word, Daniel moves toward the back bookcase. He motions for George to stand next to him. With a puzzled look on his face, George moves closer. Daniel takes out three various books. Then one at a time he replaces them.

Suddenly, the piece of floor that they are on, moves. It and the bookcase slowly turn. When the turn is done the bookcase and the floor have been replaced by an identical piece of the floor and bookcase. Daniel and George are on the other side of the wall.

On their side of the wall, they are in a similar room. The difference is that there are more tables and chairs. Daniel steps off the turntable and so does a shaky George.

"Why all of this secrecy?" Ask George. "Why couldn't we have just met in your office like this morning or just have stayed in that room?"

"Because, I want you to see my special resources."

"Is it in one of those three books that you took out and replaced?"

"No! It's some of my friends and co-workers."

Daniel sits down at the nearest table. He leans back and stretches his legs and then crosses them at the ankles.

"Have a seat George. I'm sure they'll be here soon."

George sits down. He is tense as he looks at Daniel. George begins to tap his foot on the floor.

"Aren't you worried that someone will one day find this room by accidentally pulling out those same books?"

"The only people who know about these two rooms are the people I trust. That now includes you. You'll be meeting most of the others in a few moments."

The moments pass and suddenly the only door in the room opens. In walks a group of young men and a woman wearing almost the same types of clothing. The men all have on dress shoes, docker pants, and short-sleeved white shirts. Some are wearing ties and some aren't. The woman in the group is wearing heels, a knee length skirt, and a white blouse. Daniel looks at them and counts.

"One of you is missing."

"Sea King had an emergency near Atlantis," says one of the men.

George's eyes open wide with surprise.

"Sea King! Are you telling me that these are those new heroes that have been popping up in the last few years?"

"Yes George. These are my new employees. Group this is my old friend George Kirby, but you may know him as Kid Patriot."

The group gathers around him and all are smiling. They shake his hand and greet him happily as they are in awe to meet a living legend.

"Pleased to meet you," says Barbara Brown, AKA the Brown Bolo.

"Sir, you are a living legend," Says Allen (Accelerate) Anderson.

"You are an inspiration to all of us Mr. Kirby," says Golden Guardian in his identity of Glenn Gordon.

Jubilation turns to sadness when they suddenly realize why he must be there.

"Sorry for your loss."

"He was a great man."

"We all feel for you sir."

Daniel sits down and the rest takes a seat.

"Yes he is here to tell us something about Flag-waver. Before we begin I have to ask. How did you all fit in that phone booth together?" Ask Daniel.

Atomic Sprite looks up.

"We didn't. We entered one at a time and waited at the end of the hall for each other."

"That's good but we will have to find other ways to get you all in here. All of you using an old phone booth will attract too much attention to the project."

At that moment, Sea King burst in the door. He is only wearing his trunks and dripping wet.

"Sorry, I'm late but…"

"It's ok they explained. Take a seat."

"No offense but I'm too wet to sit so I'll just stand in the corner."

"Suit yourself. The visitor is my old friend George Kirby and the former Kid Patriot."

Sea King and George start to shake hands till Daniel stops them.

"No more time for pleasant greetings. George you have the floor tell them your story."

George stands as he proceeds to tell the tale of Flag-waver. He tells it with passion, heart, and all the feeling that one can muster when talking about a recently fallen friend.

Chapter 7

Lo, The Night of Stonehenge

The night after the meeting finds Mr. Stretchable and Sea King on top of a building near the docks. They are on a stakeout watching for a villain known as Stonehenge.

"I hear you still haven't given Daniel your real name," says Sea King.

"No, not yet," replies Mr. Stretchable.

"How does he make your paycheck out to you?"

"Not really your business but if you're interested he pays me in cash. It's a temporary situation till I decide if I want to join permanently."

"Kind of like a contractor."

"Yeah, kind of."

"If you haven't even given him a fake name, what do your co-workers call you?"

"I'm in the mail room. I just sort letters. No one there bothers me and there's no need for anyone to talk to me."

"Why are you taking so long to decide? Most of us made our decisions right away."

"I'm just not in favor of one man having all that information about me. I never had to give that information to anyone once I got my powers. That knowledge could get them hurt or hurt me if that person turns against me."

"Daniel Urich was the Terror when he was younger. I doubt you have to worry about him being hurt or turning on you."

"Then there should be no problem with me not telling him anything then."

"What do you mean?"

"What I mean is that since he is a former superhero he should know better than anyone else why I don't give out my real name."

Deciding to change the subject Mr. Stretchable ask Sea King a question.

"Stonehenge is someone I've fought before. I haven't read anything in the papers that you fought him. So why do you think he's going to hit the Mariner's Bank?"

"I have some informants who told me they heard he was hitting it tonight since today was the day that most of the fishermen deposited their pay."

Suddenly a car stops in the alley next to the closed bank. Out of the car step five men. Four are in normal everyday clothing. The one whom the others are following is made entirely of stone, even the clothes he is wearing.

"There he is," says Sea King.

"I know but there's no law against parking a car. So we have to wait," says Mr. Stretchable.

Soon Stonehenge and his men move to the back of the bank. Mr. Stretchable and Sea King quietly move to another vantage point so they can get a better look.

"I wish I could help him," whispers Mr. Stretchable.

"What do you mean?" Sea King ask.

"Stonehenge was once a law-abiding archeologist but when he was at the real Stonehenge he was hit by some force that changed not only his appearance but also his mind. He started a life dedicated to crime instead of archeology."

"So you want to find a cure for him," says Sea King.

"Would that I could," replies Mr. Stretchable.

Suddenly from below Stonehenge raises his two fists and strikes the back of the wall as hard as he can. The bricks of the wall didn't stand a chance against such force and immediately crumble to dust under the force of the blows.

"We didn't have to wait long," says Stretchable.

The two heroes jump into action and enter the bank through the hole in the wall just behind Stonehenge and his gang.

"STRETCHABLE!" Yells Stonehenge.

"That's Mr. Stretchable to you rock face," he replies.

"I don't know how you and your friend found out about my plans but you won't stop us."

With that he and his men spring into action against our heroes. A battle rages on in the vault of the small bank. It ends with Mr. Stretchable wrapping his whole body around the four henchmen to hold them for the police. Stonehenge makes his escape through the hole in the wall. Stretchable looks at Sea King.

"I'm kind of tied up here right now. Can't you command a big fish or something to come out of the river and eat rock face?"

"I don't command the sea life. I am not their king. I can only ask them, but I do have command over the water."

Sea King goes out the hole and sees Stonehenge driving the getaway car down the street that runs near the ocean. Sea King closes his eyes and concentrates. As he does he silently commands the water and a huge wave rises from the ocean. Then it comes down, with pinpoint accuracy on Stonehenge's car. The power of the wave drives it into the ground. Sea King arrives on the site and Mr. Stretchable, who still has the men wrapped up in his body, arrives right behind him.

"Now I know why they call you Sea King." Says Mr. Stretchable.

"We told you that you wouldn't escape," says Sea King to Stonehenge whose head is poking through the top of the car.

"Blast it! The Blue Hun said this wouldn't happen."

Sea King is shocked at that last sentence.

"The Blue Hun! That can't be," says Sea King.

"What's the Blue Hun?" Ask Mr. Stretchable.

"The Blue Hun is an old World War II villain, one of Hitler's super soldiers. According to history, the Blue Hun is dead. It can't be the Blue Hun. What do you know about the Hun Stonehenge?"

Sea King waits for a reply, but none is coming. He looks at Stonehenge, but there is no movement.

"Yeah, that's stony. When he doesn't want to give out info he wills himself to become solid as a rock. On one hand, you won't get any information out of him anytime soon. On the other hand, it makes it easier to hand him over to the police."

With that said they all sit there and wait for the police to arrive.

Chapter 8

An Unpleasant Memory

The next day Daniel Urich is meeting at his home office with his old friend George. Greetings are exchanged. As George walks around the room he looks at the bookcases that are filled from floor to ceiling.

"Well read I see," George says.

"Can't get ahead in business or life without reading some books," Daniel says.

"So why did you call me over here?" Inquired George.

"I wanted to ask what you know about an old World War II Nazi named the Blue Hun."

"Well, Flag-waver and I faced him a time or two. He was a short, broad, hairy man who wore a blue uniform with a big swastika on the front and a blue colored metal German helmet that came to a point on the top and for him the helmet came down in front to cover the top part of his face. All you could see were those piercing red eyes from under that helmet. They said he was a super solider, but I never witnessed anything super about him. He was able to gather together people that normally you couldn't get to even agree with each other that the grass was green. I kind of doubt that Hitler could have gotten as far as he did in the war without him. Why do you ask?"

"Sea King and Mr. Stretchable stopped a bank robbery last night. The leader of the crooks mentioned his name."

"You don't think he was involved do you? After all he died in that bunker with Hitler."

"According to Sea King the crook, Stonehenge, made it sound like he had personally talked to the Blue Hun."

"I doubt it. I mean even if he survived the war he would have to be older than I am and I'm an old man."

"Just because he's old doesn't mean he couldn't have talked to him. He could be the mastermind behind the whole thing."

"Why would he? What would an old man profit from robbing a bank?"

"The same as a young man."

"I still don't think it was him," says George.

"Why not?" Ask Daniel.

"Because there was a lot of fighting going on at that bunker. I was there so I should know. He couldn't have gotten out without being killed and if he lived he would have been caught and tried for his war crimes."

"What if he wasn't even there?"

"That's possible. It was always reported that he was there as he was seen in the area. However, a lot of bodies were turned to ashes in the fires that broke out. It's always been thought that his body was amongst the ashes."

"So it is possible that he lived and is committing crimes today."

"Possible but unlikely. I still don't see a man that old bent on committing crimes or trying to take over the world."

"Well," says Daniel, "it's either that or there is a new Blue Hun."

"Maybe Stonehenge mentioned that name just to throw us off and make us think he didn't mastermind the robbery."

"Why mention the Blue Hun? Why not Fly Man or the Flapper or any other crook that's around?"

"I don't know," says George. "Maybe your employees should look into this."

"They will," says Daniel. "They will."

Chapter 9

Wanted: The Blue Hun, Dead or Alive!

Soon Daniel Urich is at the office. On the way in he stops by his secretary's desk. She is typing a letter and stops when he approaches.

"Good morning Mr. Urich," she says as she looks up from her typewriter.

"Good morning. Would you please tell Samuel King I need to speak with him. Please be discreet when telling him. It's something of a delicate nature and I only wish Mr. King to know."

"Yes sir! I understand Mr. Urich."

As he enters the office she picks up the phone. Daniel stops her.

"Not on the phone. Someone could accidentally hear on another line. Please do it in person. Try to make sure no one is listening."

"Yes sir!"

As he closes his office door his secretary gets up to get Mr. King.

Ten minutes later his intercom buzzes.

"Yes!"

"Samuel King is here to see you Mr. Urich."

"Thank you. Send him in."

The massive office doors open and in walks a nice looking but a mild-mannered man who looks to be in his late 20's.

"Have a seat Mr. King."

"Thanks, why did you ask for me?"

"I'll tell you in just a moment."

Daniel presses a button underneath the arm of his chair. From under the floor, soundproof walls rise and go all the way up to the ceiling. Once they are in place Daniel talks.

"I can't believe your real name is Sam King and you fight crime as Sea King."

"You know I didn't pick the name Sea King. Now what is this really about? I doubt it's my monthly performance review."

"No it's more serious but you should try to take more calls each hour."

"Very funny."

"I want to know if you think that the real Blue Hun is still alive?"

"He could be. I suppose you talked to George."

"Earlier this morning. He doesn't seem to fully believe it either. He says he died in Hitler's bunker and there was so much fighting going on that he would have been shot or burned alive at the bunker."

"My people live longer than those that live on land. I may look young, but I was there," says Sea King.

"I knew you were older, but I didn't think you were that much older."

"Yes as I told you I was exiled by my people. I didn't want to show that I was different from land-dwellers so I didn't show my abilities. To serve both Atlantis and the surface I enlisted in the military. George's memory seems a little faulty, after all those years. I can assure you that the most fighting was on the outskirts of Berlin as we had the city surrounded. The troops that Hitler had at that point to defend himself and the city were few and not united. With the Blue Huns ability to rally the troops Hitler would have ordered him to gather the troops if the Blue Hun were with him."

"You mean that the Blue Hun wasn't even in the city?"

"History has recorded that he died in the Bunker but, if the Hun is still alive, then the only answer is that he wasn't there," Says Sea King.

"We have to find the Hun," says Daniel.

"I'll make sure that the others know to be on the lookout for him," says Sea King.

Chapter 10

The Hunt for the Hun Begins

Later that night the Brown Bolo is on patrol. She leaps from roof to roof. One leap is slightly miscalculated and she loses her footing as she lands. She slips off and begins a fall of 20 stories. She quickly grabs a bolo from her backpack. She throws it at a fire escape on the building and holds tight to a rope that is tied to the bolo. The bolo hits the edge of the fire escape but bounces off. It starts falling back towards her.

It was the Brown Bolo's only chance and she blew it. Her thoughts quickly race through her mind of all the dangerous fights she has survived and now the news will read that she fell to her death because she didn't jump far enough or perhaps they will suspect a crook pushed her off during a fight. Either way she will be dead because this one time her aim was just slightly off.

Suddenly she stops in mid air. Her rope bolo falls next to her and stops also. It is then that she realizes she is lying on a golden platform. She looks behind her to see a yellow beam. Her eyes follow it upward to reveal the beam coming from the wrist of the Golden Guardian.

"Going down?" Ask the Guardian.

"Not by choice," says Bolo.

"You should watch your step."

"There was a time I would never be off my game," says Bolo. "Working in an office has made me soft. I should spend that time looking for crime and practicing my skills."

"Take it easy on yourself. Something like that could happen to any of us," says the Guardian.

"I bet it wouldn't happen to Mr. Stretchable," replies the Brown Bolo.

"You kind of have a thing for him don't you."

"Well, he is kind of cute but I only have eyes for you sweetheart."

Deciding to change the subject the Golden Guardian asks Bolo a question.

"Have you talked to Sea King lately?"

"Yeah and that's the reason for my patrol tonight."

"The hunt for the Hun."

"Careful honey, or some people will think that the grim Golden Guardian has a sense of humor."

Just then, a woman's scream is heard from down the street.

"What was that?" Ask the Guardian.

"We better investigate."

Guardian picks up the Brown Bolo and they fly till they see the screaming woman. They are about to land but don't when she looks up and sees them. She points to a man running away and shouts to them.

"He just stole my purse."

With that, they fly off into the night sky in pursuit of the thief.

"Great!" Thinks the thief. "Now I have a couple of superheroes after me. I'd give myself up, but this would be my third time in prison. Maybe I'll get lucky and they won't catch me."

But luck isn't on his side. He turns down an alley to hide from view, but he can't hide from the Golden Guardian. A yellow wall appears in front of the thief. He turns to run back the way he came when he is wrapped up tight by a bolo that comes from above. Then our two heroes land in front of the thief.

"If it isn't Jake the Snake," says the Brown Bolo.

"Don't you have more things to do than harass me, Bolo?"

"Yes but you keep committing crimes that I have to stop."

"Give me the purse," commands the Golden Guardian.

Jake, knowing he can't escape, releases the purse from his grip and the Guardian takes it.

"You know anything about a crook called the Blue Hun?" Ask Bolo.

"That World War II relic! I thought he was dead."

"You know Jake," says the Guardian. "I can use my band to tell if you're lying."

"Look I've heard some old-timers mention the name but I just thought they were thinking about old times."

"Jake I know if we make a citizen's arrest that it would be your third time in jail," says Bolo.

"You should. You sent me there the last two times."

"Since you've returned the purse we can just let you go if you promise to keep yourself clean and let us know if you hear anymore about the Blue Hun."

Unseen by the Brown Bolo the Golden Guardian, who is standing behind her, gives her a disapproving look.

"That's all and I go free?"

"That's all."

"You've got a deal."

With that, the Brown Bolo takes off the bolo that has him tied up and Jake takes off.

"Do you really think he is going to stop committing crimes and will ever tell us about the Blue Hun?" Ask the Golden Guardian.

"Maybe not, but this way he has a chance to stay straight and we have someone else to help us look for the Hun."

With that the Guardian picks her up and they fly off to return the purse to the woman down the street.

Chapter 11

Sick Days

The next day Daniel Urich is in his office. Suddenly his door burst open. Michael Hacker, a manager for the Urich Foundation, rushes in. He is followed by Daniel's secretary.

"What's going on here?" Inquired Daniel.

"I'm sorry Mr. Urich but I told Mr. Hacker he had to wait. But he ignored me and came in any way," answers his Secretary.

"I got a lot of work to do to Daniel and only half the staff you gave me to do it." Says Mr. Hacker.

"It's okay. I'll speak with Mr. Hacker even though he didn't have an appointment."

With that, she turns and leaves and closes the door behind her. Michael Hacker walks up to Daniel's desk and leans forward on it with both hands.

"It's like I said Mr. Urich. I have a lot of work to do and I thought it would be a breeze to get through when you doubled my team. But almost every day someone is calling in sick. Instead of reporting these sick days like normal, I have to report them directly to you. My team isn't getting its work done any faster and all the paperwork I have to fill out is taking up more of my time so I have to stay later to finish my work. If I were to report these sick days in the normal fashion, most of these new people would have used them all up by now. What is going on? My family hardly sees me now. If I'm going be spending this much time at work. I think I deserve to know what is going on."

" Michael, I wish I could tell you, but the time isn't right. Just know that your work on this is not going unnoticed by me. You're doing a great service for the community. I can't promise you that it will end anytime soon. Why don't you take the rest of the day off, correction, take the rest of the week off, and see your family starting now."

Michael Hacker takes a step back and looks shocked. He thinks his boss has mistaken his concern for his work as anger towards his employer.

"Mr. Urich, I'm sorry if I've upset you. I'm just concerned about the work getting done."

"Michael first let me say this. We've known each other a long time so when we talk in private like this you can call me Daniel, now let me assure you that your job is not in danger. I can tell you're stressed and need time off. Take a few days and take your family somewhere. The time will be with pay. Your job will be back here next week when you get back. Now, is there any other reason you came to see me?"

"Yes, I came to tell you that Vincent Valentine had called in sick for the fifth day in a row."

Later that night on the other side of town Jake "the snake" enters a rundown bar. To his left are two pool tables with two men at each table playing a game. To his right are four tables only the table in the corner has one man seated at the table. He has a drink and a hamburger on the table in front of him. Only one bite is taken out of the hamburger and the drink looks like it hasn't been touched. Jake walks up to the bar across from the doorway. There is a huge mirror on the wall behind the bar that is so dirty it looks like it hasn't been washed in months. It has so many cracks and pieces of glass missing that he can hardly see anything in it. The bartender is a muscular looking man with a black T-shirt on. He scratches his bald head as he approaches Jake.

"So Jake what do you want?" Ask the bartender.

"Just give me the usual." Answers Jake.

As the bartender moves to the other side of the bar to get Jake his usual drink two of the men at one of the pool tables stop their game. With pool cues still in hand, they both stand on either side of Jake.

"So where ya been?" Ask the man on Jake's right side.

"Just around, nowhere special." Replies Jake.

"I heard you got caught stealing a purse last night." Says the man on Jake's left side.

Jake starts to feel a little nervous. Why would they care if he got caught stealing a purse? He thinks to himself.

"Yeah, so what?"

"So why would the cops let you go?" Ask the man on the left.

"I don't know. I was just told if I returned it. I could go."

"These wouldn't be special cops would they?" Questioned the man on the right.

"What do you mean special cops?"

"You know, I mean, they weren't those superheroes, like say the Brown Bolo and the Golden Guardian?"

Now Jake really is nervous. How could they know exactly who they were? He didn't see anybody around last night. He knows he has to answer their question but can't seem afraid.

"Yeah, so what if it was?"

"So what?" Says the man on the left. "Because a purse is small time for two like that. Why would they team up to catch a purse snatcher unless they wanted something bigger?"

"Maybe they were just feeling kind last night."

The bartender brings Jake his drink. Jake takes his drink and starts to move away from the bar towards one of the empty tables. Suddenly, before he can take his next step, the man on the left grabs both of Jake's arms and holds them behind Jake. Jake drops his drink on the floor. The other man steps in front of Jake.

"I think you do know says the man standing in front of Jake. And you are going to tell us."

The man takes a couple of steps back then takes the pool cue, holds a like a baseball bat and swings and hits Jake in the face. When Jake looks up his nose is bleeding.

"I will ask you again, what did they want from you?"

"Nothing!"

The man hits Jake again with the pool cue, but this time it breaks. So then he repeatedly hit Jake in the stomach and the face with his fist. When Jake drops to the floor, the other man lets him go and joins in on the beating. All this time the bartender, the other two men at the pool table, and the man in the corner do nothing but watch. Finally, Jake can take no more. The beating stops. Jake looks up. His face is a bloody mess. He tries to stand to his feet but cannot. Finally, he says two words, Blue Hun.

"What did they want to know about the Blue Hun?" Ask one of the men.

"They just wanted to know if I knew or heard of anything about the Blue Hun."

"What did you tell them?"

"Nothing because I don't know anything."

"We'll make sure it stays that way."

The two men get closer to Jake. Both start to raise their fists to start beating him again. Suddenly they find themselves lifted in midair. They turn their heads to see they're both being held by the man who was seated at the corner table. He takes them to the door of the bar and throws them out. Then he goes back to Jake and picks him up with both hands and carries him out the door. He leaves the men at the pool table and the bartender standing there in shock.

Outside the bar, he stands holding Jake in his arms. The other two men have already left. While he stands there motionless holding Jake's body his appearance starts to change. When the change is complete, we see that the man is really the Venusian Visionary in disguise. Silently he flies away as he carries Jake to the nearest hospital.

Chapter 12

Behold...The Visionary!

Later that night at Daniel Urich's estate Louis is finishing his rounds to make sure everything is okay before goes to bed. Suddenly in the foyer he sees an eerie blue glow. As he goes to take a look to see what it is, he picks up an empty vase in case he needs to use it as a weapon. As he enters the foyer he raises the vase into the air. He does not strike the intruder as to his amazement floating there above the ground is the Venusian Visionary.

Louis is shocked but relieved that it is a friend of Daniel's that has arrived. He knows that there is no need to ask how he got into a locked house that is equipped with the latest in home security as the Venusian Visionary has the power to teleport himself anywhere he wants.

"You are Louis are you not?" Ask the Venusian Visionary.

"I am. May I ask the reason for your visit?" Inquired Louis.

"I need to speak with Daniel."

"I will let him know you're here Sir."

"There's no need of that. I can sense where he is and he seems to know that I'm already here."

With that being said, the Visionary abruptly disappears only to reappear in front of Daniel Urich. Daniel is above his mansion in a hidden attic that he once used as his headquarters when he was more active as the Terror. Now, as the Terror, he only uses it from time to time. Other times he uses it as a quiet room where he can go to read. Right now, he is seated in front of a table where we can see he has been reading the Bible that is lying on the table in front of him. As he looks up at the glowing blue figure he shows no signs of surprise to see his superpowered friend there.

"Hello Vincent! I thought I would be seeing you tonight since you have been out of the office for a week." Says Daniel.

"Yes, I have some information. Also, I prefer not to be called Vincent when in my natural form since that is not my real name."

"Well, I don't think Venusian Visionary is your real name either, but as you wish."

Visionary tells Daniel what happened at the bar. He informs him that he took Jake to the hospital and left him there. He also tells him how he read Jake's mind and that Jake has no insurance and has no information on the Blue Hun.

"Why didn't you stop the beating if you could read his mind?" Ask Daniel.

"I didn't want to give away my identity. I stepped in when I saw they wished to kill him," says Visionary.

"Well, now those two thugs must know that we are on to them. Obviously they have information or work for the Blue Hun."

"Shall we inform the others to be on the lookout for these two and follow them?" Ask the Visionary.

"No! I have a feeling that we'll be hearing from them very soon." Answers Daniel. "Also, stay informed about Jake's health. I'll put the funds in your account so you can pay for his hospital bill."

Chapter 13

The Villains Lair

In another part of town are the two men whom Daniel and the Venusian Visionary were talking about. They're walking down a street lined with old buildings. They stop in front of one building and check to make sure that no one sees them. They walk around to the back and open a wooden door. Then they walk down a staircase that is made of wood but halfway down changes to steel. At the end of that staircase is another door. Like the last half of the staircase, the door is also made of steel. They each press their thumbs to a button. The readout above says," Fingerprint, scan complete. You may enter." The door quickly slides open. Once the second man is past the doorway, the door quickly slides shut.

The room is almost barren. Just four metal walls, two chairs and the metal doors on the two far end walls.

"We never seem to get beyond this room," says the first man.

"What he pays us for these tests, I don't need to go into the next room," says the second man.

Suddenly a computerized voice fills the room.

"Welcome, gentlemen! I see our last experiment wasn't able to enhance your strength."

"That's right, but how did you know that? I thought we had to report back and tell you," says the first man.

"This experiment is very important to me. I have my ways of finding things out. I can't rely on just your word alone."

"So is the money going to be directly deposited to our accounts?" Ask the second man.

"You'll see it in your Swiss bank accounts that I had set up for you tomorrow. I also understand you took care of someone who was looking for me."

"Yeah, some crook. Everyone calls Jake the snake," says the first man.

"But this Jake the snake knows nothing of my experiments. Why would you bring attention to him?"

"He was an informant for the Brown Bolo and the Golden Guardian. If he found anything out he would've told them," says the second man.

"So you did this to send a message to the Brown Bolo and the Golden Guardian."

"Yeah right!"

"YOU SENT A MESSAGE TO TWO SUPERHEROES BY BEATING UP A MAN WHO KNEW NOTHING OF MY OPERATION! HE WOULD NOT HAVE FOUND OUT ANYTHING! NOW INSTEAD OF GIVING UP, THEY AND MAYBE OTHERS, WILL CONTINUE TO LOOK FOR ME!" Shouts the computerized voice.

"We're sorry," says the first man.

"Yeah, we thought we were helping you," says the second man.

"No need to worry. I can take care of any trouble that comes my way. But thank you for your concern. Would you both be willing to take another test? For say an extra $5,000 each."

"Sure!" Both men say in unison.

Upon their agreement, a metal table slides out from the wall next to them. On the table are two capsules with a clip on each of them.

"Clip the two capsules to your belt," says the voice.

The two men take the capsules and clip them to their belts just as the voice directed.

"These capsules are to enhance your stamina. If the enhancement is successful nothing short of a tank should be able to take you down."

Suddenly from each capsule comes two small metal arms that poke through each man's shirt and injects itself under their skin. Each man winces as he feels a little bit of pain.

"There may be some pain at first, but if the experiment is a success you won't feel the pain much longer."

With that, the two men turned to leave. The door they came in slides open and as the last man leaves it quickly slides closed.

Chapter 14

Death Be Not Proud!

It's lunchtime and two co-workers from the Urich Foundation, Allen Anderson and Adam Stevenson, are eating at Big Burger, the fast food restaurant close to where they work.

The place is packed with the midday rush. The line is almost going out the door. Allen and Adam have just gotten their orders. Allen is already seated and Adam is approaching him with a tray of food.

"You must be very hungry. I never saw anyone rush to a table so fast once he got his food," says Adam as he takes his seat.

"I am. Everyone moves so slow at work I run around helping everyone with their work when I finish mine," replies Allen.

"I haven't said anything Al but you're not helping. It doesn't bother me, but some of the others think you're trying to show them up," says Adam.

"They're getting mad at me?"

"Yep!"

Allen is already half way through his sandwich, but Adam is starting to take his first bite. Suddenly Allen grabs Adams arm.

"I know you're hungry but you can't have my sandwich."

"It's not that. Remember those two guys behind us in line?"

"Yeah, why?"

"One of them is reaching for something. I think it's a gun."

Suddenly the young man in front of the cashier does pull out a gun. The young man next to him pulls out a bag and throws it to the cashier.

"Fill that bag with all the money," says the man with the gun.

"No one go anywhere. We'll pass the bag to the rest of you to fill with your money," says the other man.

The only ones who seem to be gone are Allen and Adam as their table is empty. Only their food is left behind.

Suddenly, the man with the gun sees his gun ripped out of his hand by an unseen force. Before everyone's eyes, it hovers in mid-air and the bullets magically fall out of the gun.

"What is going on here?" He ask.

"I am!" Says Accelerate as he seems to appear from nowhere.

Accelerate uses his super speed and with his fist continues to punch the crook in the stomach. The man just stands there and takes it with a smile.

In front of the second crook, almost unnoticed by the naked eye seems to float a small fly. But this unusually colored fly of bright red and yellow gets very aggressive and strikes the man in the jaw. The man flinches. The little fly grows to the size of a man and reveals himself to be the Atomic Sprite.

"Interrupt my lunch will you?" Says the Atomic Sprite.

He hits the man again on the right side of his face. Then again on the left side. But the crook just stands there and smiles. Before another blow can be struck they hear a police siren.

"We better get out of here," says the first man.

They both run out the door leaving our two heroes amazed at what just happened.

"How could they just stand there and take that?" Ask Accelerate.

"I know. I kept hitting harder each time and he just stood there and smiled."

"I'll see if I can catch them."

Accelerate runs out the door. In a second he comes back.

"Sprite you better see this."

He picks up Atomic Sprite and runs into an alley where he puts him down. As he gets his legs under him Sprite sees two dead bodies of a couple of old men.

"So what happened to them? Did they try to stop the crooks?" He ask Accelerate.

"Take a closer look. Notice anything familiar about them?"

"Oh my gosh! They're wearing the same type of clothes as those two crooks."

"It's more than just the clothes. I think they are the two crooks."

"WHAT!!! How could they age 50 years in just two minutes?"

"I don't know but it must be them. They have on the same clothes and are the same size as the crooks."

The two just stand there shocked at what they believe to be true. They try to make sense of what they are looking at.

"You know," says Atomic Sprite, "so we can find a way to make sense of this and find out if what we suspect is true, we need to get these bodies back to the Foundation before anyone else finds them."

"You're right!" Replies Accelerate.

He bends down and picks up both bodies and holds one over each shoulder. Then Atomic Sprite shrinks down to the size of an insect. He jumps up on the back of one of the bodies. Then he holds on for dear life to the dead man's shirt as Accelerate takes off at top speed toward the Foundation.

Chapter 15

A Clear and Deadly Power

Deep in a sub-basement of the Foundation Daniel, Accelerate and Atomic Sprite use the advanced medical equipment that Daniel has to examine the two bodies.

"I've run every test I can but don't see anything to show that these were young men only moments ago," says Daniel.

"There must be some way to prove it," says Accelerate.

"Maybe they're just two old guys who were dressed the same as the guys you were after," says Daniel.

"I don't think so. That would be too much a coincidence," says Sprite.

"Maybe another member of our team can help." Says Accelerate.

"Who did you have in mind?" Ask Sprite.

"Golden Guardian."

"We may also need Visionary," says Daniel.

Daniel picks up a phone. He only dials two numbers.

"Mr. Hacker please have Vincent Valentine and Glenn Gordon meet me in my office."

With that he hangs up the phone. He then turns to face the others.

"I'll have them here in a few moments."

With that Daniel went to the only elevator in the basement. It led directly to his office and was only accessed to behind his massive bookcase. He pressed the button. The doors closed. Then two massive jets on the bottom of the elevator activated and took him straight up to his office in a matter of seconds.

True to his word in less than five minutes Daniel was back with Visionary and Guardian in their civilian identities.

"Gentlemen," says Daniel. "Accelerate and Atomic Sprite says that these two men aged prematurely. We have used all that science has to offer and come up with nothing. Can you two please examine them and tell us if you come up with anything?"

With that request, Glenn Gordon activates his powerful wristband and Vincent Valentine closes his eyes places both hands on the side of his head.

Slowly their clothes disappear and are replaced by the uniforms of the Golden Guardian and the Venusian Visionary.

Guardian uses his band as a yellow beam emits from it and envelopes both bodies. Visionary just stands there and stares at both bodies. It would seem to most that he isn't doing anything. However, small beads of sweat start to appear on his forehead. Almost at the same time Guardian retracts his beam just as Visionary collapses into a chair.

"Did you find out anything?" Ask Daniel.

"Yes!" Says Guardian. "There is massive cellular damage to both men. It's like they stood up to too much stress in a very short period of time. It is possible that they aged rapidly."

"He is correct," says Visionary. "It takes a lot of strength to read the memories of just one dead man. This was very difficult to read that of two. I can say without a doubt that they were young earlier in the day."

"What could have happened to do this?" Ask Daniel.

"I don't know," says Visionary. "But these are the two men who put Jake the Snake in the hospital."

"Who's Jake the Snake?" Ask Sprite.

"He was the Bolo's eyes and ears on the street to get information on the Blue Hun," says the Guardian.

"What does this have to do with the Blue Hun?" Questioned Accelerate.

"Visionary! What else did you see in their memories?" Ask Daniel.

"Not much. They had meetings with someone who they called the Blue Hun, but I couldn't see if they knew who the Hun is or what the Hun's plans are."

"So Stonehenge is robbing for him and these two are beating up people and dying for him," says the Guardian.

"What is going on here?" Ask Sprite.

"I don't know yet," says Daniel. "We're only seeing small pieces of a very big picture. One thing I do know is that I'm going to have to tell George."

Chapter 16

Dead Men Tell Tales

Later that night Daniel is at his home and having dinner with George. They're seated at a 15 foot long table in an enormous dining room. The room is made completely of dark wood. There is a suit of armor standing in each corner of the room. A beautiful stone fireplace is on the back wall behind Daniel with a blazing fire going. While the long table stretches the length of the room. Both men find it more convenient to sit just at one end. They have just finished their dinner and Louis has come to take the plates away. As Louis walks out the door to take the plates to the kitchen George looks at Daniel.

"Well, that dinner was nice, but you sounded like you had something more on your mind than just wanting to have company at mealtime. What's on your mind?"

"Flag-waver trained you well. I thought I did my best to hide my real emotions from you over the phone." Replies Daniel.

"You put on a pretty good act, but there were certain inflections that I still picked up on," says George.

"I won't insult your intelligence anymore George. I'll just put it bluntly we've gotten information that the Blue Hun is still alive."

"That, I already know."

"We think he's conducting experiments?"

"What makes you think that?"

"Accelerate and Atomic Sprite stopped two young small time robbers. They tried to get away and they followed them. When they found them, these two young men were dead of old age. Golden Guardian confirmed it and Visionary read their memories."

"What did visionary undercover?"

"He found out that they were two men with connections to the Blue Hun. They were also the two men that he had stopped from killing Jake the snake."

At that point, George stands and starts pacing on his side of the table. He stops in front of a suit of armor and stares at it. Without turning around, he asks Daniel a question.

"What kind of experiments is he conducting?"

"We're not sure but we believe it involves testing the stamina of the people."

"Was anything found on the bodies?"

"Nothing unusual that I noticed."

"Would you mind if I took a look at the bodies?"

"I wouldn't mind. But we'll have to turn the bodies over to the police soon." Replies Daniel.

"Then we better be going," says George.

With that, both men walk out of the dining room. Daniel sees Louis and tells him to bring the car around. They're going to the Foundation.

Moments later Daniel and George are in the secret subbasement of the Foundation. They're standing in front of the two bodies that Daniel had placed in a special case that would stop decomposition.

"Are you ready for this?" Ask Daniel.

"I've seen dead bodies before," replies George.

With that, Daniel presses a button. The lids of the cases slide back to reveal the bodies. George slowly looks in but soon is almost crawling into the case. He begins feeling around the waist of both of the dead men.

"What are you looking for?" Ask Daniel.

"It's been a long time so I won't be quite sure unless I find it," replies George.

Suddenly a look of surprise mixed with sadness crosses over George's face. He pulls something off the side of one of the men. As he does it tears off a couple of small pieces of the man's skin. George gets out of the case and shows his finding to Daniel.

"This is what I was looking for," says George.

"I saw that earlier, but I thought it was part of the belt," says Daniel.

"That's understandable," says George." There were two of these on each man and they clipped onto the belt and they did look a lot like they were part of the belt. If you look close you can see there are very thin pieces of threadlike wires. Unless you're looking for them you would miss them. They injected under the person's skin. This would increase the human beings stamina. But it was only supposed to be a temporary injection. They were supposed to just quickly get you and then retract.

For some reason, these stayed injected into these men. It increased their stamina but cost them to quickly burn out and die of old age."

"How did you know to look for that?" Ask Daniel.

"Flag-waver told me that whenever he felt like he couldn't go on anymore something from his belt would come out and quickly sting him. Suddenly he would feel rejuvenated and was able to continue the fight. I didn't know for sure that it was on these men, but I had to check."

"So these are from Flag-waver's cosmic belt?"

"No! The belt could not be disassembled."

"The Blue Hun has been trying to make his own belt so that it can be disassembled?"

"It looks that way doesn't it," says George.

"To do that he would have to have a model to work from," says Daniel.

"I know. This means that the Blue Hun just might have the original cosmic belt."

Chapter 17

Bar Room Brawl

The next night at the bar, where Jake the Snake nearly met his end, there are two new customers. One is already standing at the bar when the other comes in. He walks up to the bar and orders his drink.

"Pepsi."

"And?" Ask the bartender.

"And what?" Ask the new customer.

"What other drink. No one comes into a bar and orders just a soft drink."

"Look buddy I'm on the wagon. I was passing by and I was thirsty so I just want a soft drink."

"Ok!" Says the bartender as he holds his hands up in resignation. "I just wanted to make sure."

As he turns to get his customer his drink two other men from a nearby table approach the customer.

"So you can't handle your drink," says one of the men.

"Not much of a man who can't drink," says the other.

"Listen guys I just wanted something to drink. I didn't want any trouble."

The first man looks him right in the eye. He gets his face close enough that their noses almost touch.

"Buddy I just wanted to talk," he says. "But if you want trouble I can give it to you."

From the other end of the bar, the other customer comes to his aid. He pushes back his hat and looks over at them.

"He just told you he didn't want any trouble."

Slowly both men turn their attention to the new customer. They both step slowly in his direction.

"Well, maybe he doesn't want any trouble," says the first man.

"But you're the one that found it," says the other.

Both men start to attack the man, but only one does. The other is held back by the other customer.

The first man pounds furiously at the customer but stops. He looks at him not believing that he is still standing.

"I've nearly broken both hands on you and you still haven't fallen."

The customer just smiles. Then he grabs the man and throws him into the corner of the bar.

The other man finally breaks free of the hold that the non-drinking customer had him in. He turns to the man who held him prisoner and begins to pound on him too but with the same results.

"Who are you two?" He asks as he turns and runs out the door.

The two men turn their attention back to the bar. The bartender brings two soft drinks and puts them in front of them.

"They're on the house. Those two are always chasing off customers. I never knew how to get rid of them."

As they quickly down their drinks one looks at the other.

"A Pepsi?"

"Like I said, I don't drink and it got some results," whispers the other man.

Just then, a customer from another table gets up and approaches them. He stops at the bar and turns to face them both.

"That was an impressive show you two put on."

"That wasn't show. That was survival."

"Either way that was impressive. If you two are looking for work go to this address. I think you will work out just fine," he says as he hands them a card.

"What kind of work?"

"Just show up there and you'll find out."

They each take a card and both walk out of the bar together. They walk down the street into the black of the night. No one is around so they both change back to their real identities of the Venusian Visionary and Mr. Stretchable.

"I thought you were supposed to be pliable," says Visionary.

"I can also make myself as hard as you if I wish," replies Mr. Stretchable.

"We'll, have to see if this address is connected to the Blue Hun," says Visionary as he looks at the card.

Chapter 18

R.S.V.P. to Doom

Later, in the secret room beneath the foundation and the streets of the city, our heroes meet to discuss your next plan of attack. Daniel is seated at the desk in the center of the room. Standing around him in a circle are the other superheroes. They have just finished discussing the undercover work that was done by Visionary and Stretchable.

"Do you think this has anything to do with the Blue Hun?" Ask Daniel.

"I do believe we're on the right track." Replies Visionary.

"Well, how do we find out if the Hun is involved?" Ask the Brown Bolo.

"We need to get someone on the inside," says the Golden Guardian.

"So we should send Visionary and Stretchable back undercover?" Ask Atomic Sprite.

"That sounds good to me. But we only need one deep undercover." Says Daniel.

"Which one?" Ask Mr. Stretchable.

"We'll figure that out while we design our plan of attack," says Daniel.

The next evening a lone figure in blue jeans, a tee shirt, and an orange jacket approaches a rundown building. He stops in front of the building holding a piece of paper in his hand. Then he walks around to the back and opens a wood door. He then walks down a staircase that is made of wood that changes halfway down to steel. At the end of that staircase is another door. Like the last half of the staircase, the door is also made of steel. He presses his thumbs to a button. A voice comes from a speaker.

"Who are you?"

"My name is Vincent. I was given a card last night and told to come here."

"Look at the camera and show me the card."

Vincent looks up into the right corner and he shows the card. Suddenly the door slides open and Vincent enters. Once inside the sparse room the door closes. Vincent sees two chairs. He takes off his jacket and places it on the back of the chair and then sits down on the other.

"Why are you here?" Says the voice from the speaker.

"I need money and I need it fast. I was told that the work here paid well."

"I was told there would be two of you."

"The other guy didn't need the money as bad as I do."

"Alright, wait for a moment."

Vincent just sits there. He examines every part of the room from where he is to see if there is anything that will show if the Blue Hun is involved. Suddenly from the wall slides a panel with a tube on it.

"Clip that onto your belt," says the voice on the speaker.

Vincent takes the tube. He looks at it carefully. Then he clips it to his belt as told.

"Why am I going to get paid for just doing this?"

"You'll find out. It's best to not ask too many questions. I will set up a Swiss bank account where you can access your money. You will get $1000 for this job and more if you wish to stay on."

With that the door that he came in opens.

"Does this mean I have to go?" Ask Vincent.

But the only answer is silence. Vincent quietly turns to leave and walks out the door. However, he never picked up his jacket and it is no longer on the back of the chair. It is nowhere in the room at all.

Chapter 19

A Spy Among Us

Deep inside the sub-basement of the old run down building is a vast state of the art laboratory. Two men dressed in uniforms are sitting at a control panel monitoring a situation in the next room. Things are pretty slow so there is some time for conversation.

"These tests are pretty rough," says the first man.

"Well, they must be able to take it. They are the only ones to survive the primary first test," says the second man.

"Do you really think the Hun can get this country back on the right track?"

"Of course I do. You better be careful what you say. If the Hun suspected that you had any doubts that would be the end of you."

"You're right but I don't have any doubts. I just wanted to know what you thought."

Suddenly, the room lights up with a red glow and a siren goes off. Both men snap to attention.

"Oh no! The Hun may have both of our heads. We may lose that guy on the left."

"We need to get in there and get him out of that harness."

Both men jump up and run out of the room. Unnoticed by them in their rush they pass by an orange box. Once they are out of the room the box begins to shimmer and shake. Soon it unravels itself to reveal that it was Mr. Stretchable in disguise.

"I thought they would never leave," thinks Mr. Stretchable to himself.

"At least I now know that the Blue Hun is here and keeps them in check with fear for their lives."

He kneels next to the control panel. Then he stretches his neck so he can just peak above the panel. He sees through a window into the next room. There he sees the two men enter and head towards two other men strapped down in harnesses. The one on the left side has a look of pain on his face. The one on the right seems to be unconscious.

They rush to the man on the left. They are intent on their job as they release him from his harness.

"I better report this back to the group. Good thing that Daniel gave me this communicator."

He takes it out of a pocket and whispers into it.

"Stretch here reporting in."

Back at their secret headquarters   Daniel Urich and George Kirby are seated at a desk facing each other. They are surrounded by the group of heroes. Daniel picks up his communicator.

"Urich here. What do you have to report?"

Mr. Stretchable tells what his undercover mission has revealed. He tells that the Blue Hun is there and how test are being run on men but not sure why.

"Why would they still be running tests? Aren't those capsules enough?" Ask Sea King.

Visionary holds up the capsule that he had attached to his belt. The wires that came out of it are all bent and misshapen.

"I examined this capsule and it would seem that, if I were an ordinary human, it would have enhanced my strength. Being that the two men who fought Atomic Sprite and Accelerate were given enhanced stamina, it would seem that…"

"They are trying to give those men the powers that Flag-waver had," says George as he interrupts Visionary.

"So it would seem," says Daniel.

"I doubt that those men are there just because they are afraid," says George.

"Why?" Ask Daniel.

"I think I know what he means," says the Golden Guardian.

"Care to explain?" Ask the Brown Bolo.

"Stretchable says that they thought the Blue Hun could get the country back on the right track. The Hun must have spoken to a misguided sense of patriotism that they have."

Brown Bolo just looks at him and smiles. What Guardian has said has poked through her grim façade. She tries to fade into the background to hide her embarrassment.

"Stretchable do you have anything else to tell us?" Ask Daniel into the communicator.

They wait but no reply comes.

"Stretchable! Stretchable!" Screams Daniel.

"Still no answer," says Sea King.

"We have to assume that they have found him," says Daniel.

"You guys better go get him," says George.

"Give me a moment to get ready," says Daniel.

"GET READY?" They all ask in unison.

"Of course. He is one of my men. I'd go in to get back any one of you," says Daniel.

Daniel leaves the room for a few minutes. Later when he returns he is in his identity of the Terror. As he leads the way his black cape flaps in the breeze that he leaves in his wake and the others start to follow.

"Aren't you coming George?" Ask Accelerate.

"No, I'm too old for this. Besides someone has to stay here in case Mr. Stretchable tries to call back."

As they all leave George shakes their hands and wishes them all good luck. Then he sits back down at the table and hopes to hear from Stretchable.

As they leave Visionary looks a little upset. Sea King notices.

"Why so disturbed?"

"As I shook George's hand I got a vision."

"What kind of vision?"

"All I can say is that George Kirby may think he is sitting out this fight but he will somehow become involved."

Chapter 20

Stretched to His Limit

A few minutes earlier back on Mr. Stretchable's end of the communicator. He hears them call to him and is about to answer, but a voice from behind stops him.

"So I've been found out."

He turns around to see beautiful blonde haired, blue eyed woman in blue full-length jumpsuit. On either side of her are two guards in green jumpsuits. Each has a gun pointed at him.

"Actually it looks like I have been found out," says Mr. Stretchable. "So what are you three suppose to be? A dance troupe for the NRA?"

"Your feeble attempts at humor do not impress me."

"You still haven't answered my question."

"You really don't know do you? I AM THE BLUE HUN!"

Mr. Stretchable's jaw literally hits the floor at that revelation. His grip grows slack and he drops the communicator on the floor. The Hun motions to her men.

"Take him to the lab. We have been trying our experiments on making normal men super. Let's see what happens when we try the experiments on someone who already has super powers."

With that the guards step behind him. Suddenly, Mr. Stretchable stretches both his arms out behind him and wraps them around both men. With one hand he also disarms the man on his left. However, he isn't quick enough to disarm the man on the right. That man presses a trigger on his gun. A laser goes out of it instead of a bullet and strikes him. This shot proves the man's dedication to the Blue Hun's cause. It not only knocks out Mr. Stretchable but also the two men in his grasp.

The previous two lab technicians come back in the room. They are surprised to see what has happened in their absence.

"Where have you been?" Ask the Blue Hun.

"We were releasing a test subject because the experiment was going bad," Says one of the technicians.

"If I hadn't gotten here when I did you would have wished you were one of those test subjects."

She looks down on the three bodies. Mr. Stretchable's arms have already started to contract back to normal. He has already released the two men from his grip.

"Check those two." Says the Blue Hun as she points to the two guards.

Each tech goes to one guard. They check for any signs of life.

"He's ok!" They both say in unison.

"Good then take this one to the lab as a replacement for the one you released."

Each tech takes an arm of Mr. Stretchable's and drag him out of the room. Once they walk out the Blue Hun picks up Mr. Stretchable's communicator.

"I think we'll be having company very soon," she says as she looks at the communicator.

Chapter 21

The Underground Melee

In about twenty minutes, our heroes have arrived outside the rundown building that is just above the headquarters of the Blue Hun. They stand as a group in front of the building.

"So this is the building that you and Stretchable were led to," says the Terror.

"Yes!" Says Visionary. "There is a room down below. I saw it with my eyes, but I could see that it was much larger than one room."

"Howmuchlarger… eh… I mean… How much larger? Can you see where Mr. Stretchable is?" Ask Accelerate.

Visionary closes his eyes and concentrates. His face grows more determined. The strain is starting to take its toll. Beads of sweat form on his forehead. Suddenly his eyes open and he nearly collapses from lack of strength.

"I did my best but learned very little. I didn't learn the details of the layout, but I did see that Mr. Stretchable was being held in some type of harness."

"We need to get in there fast then if his cover was blown. How did you get in?" Ask the Terror.

Visionary leads them around the back. They stand in the almost bare backyard in a V formation.

"It was through that door that we entered," says Visionary as he points to the door on the back of the building.

Unknown to them a surveillance camera is hidden in the corner of the building. From her hidden lair deep below, the Blue Hun is watching.

"Rank amateurs being led by the senile old coot the Terror. This will be easier than I thought."

With the press of a button, a signal goes out of her control board and up to the surface. It hits several other computers and electrical triggers along the way and they too send out other signals. All of that took place in a fraction of a second. The maze of electrical waves finally culminates just below the surface of our heroes. The end result is that the ground suddenly opens up below them and seems to swallow them.

They are only half surprised as they slide down below the ground. The Terror is the last to fall. His cape snags on something above. Yet an instant later it frees itself due to the gravitational pull of the weight of the Terror's falling body. Above them, the ground is suddenly replaced.

Suddenly our group arrives at the end of their slide. They arrive in a huge room with a thud.

"Did you know this would happen?" The Brown Bolo ask Visionary.

"No, I did not. I have to be in close proximity to someone to get a clear vision. I was lucky to see anything about Mr. Stretchable."

"George, do you read me?" Says the Terror into his communicator.

From miles away George Kirby runs to the control panel. He picks up a microphone and presses a button.

"Yes Terror I read you."

"George we are…"

Suddenly the Blue Hun presses another button. All outside communications are now shut off.

"George, what happened? George!"

"Now, now, no communicating with the outside for help," Says the Blue Hun over an intercom into the room.

Miles away George is worried. He wonders what happened to the Terror and his new friends.

"Terror? Are you there? Terror?"

He waits for a reply. None will ever come.

"Something happened to them. The police will never believe me, but I have to help somehow. I can't just sit here and wait," thinks George.

With that thought, George Kirby's look goes from worried to determine. He then walks out and closes the door.

A few miles away our heroes listen to a demented Blue Hun. She is ranting on about the world and how most people don't deserve to live and how Hitler had the right ideas.

"You're insane!" Says the Terror.

"Am I? You're the heroes for your cause and you walked into an easy trap. I'd say that makes you all too stupid to live. But I also believe in giving you a chance. All of you with your special abilities, against my team of men with special abilities. Winner takes all."

With that, a wall slides up to reveal a team of superhuman men. Each one has a special clip on their belts like the ones that Accelerate and Atomic Sprite faced earlier and all of them look angry and ready for a fight.

In a matter of seconds, our heroes are attacked. A wild mêlée of a fight ensues. Each man shows signs of superhuman strength and stamina. Brown Bolo continues to throw her trick bolo's at the same man who just laughs them all off. Golden Guardian comes to her aid. He strikes from above with his power beam from his wrist. It only distracts the man. Another man sneaks up and grabs Bolo from behind. He tosses her with little effort into the air. She crashes into the Guardian and they both fall to the ground.

Similar scenes are played out with the others. The Terror uses his head and tries to stay out of reach but is grabbed from behind. His opponent is trying to strangle the life out of him. Visionary is flying above and sees this. He comes to his friend's aid, but dive bombing the enemy. His arms outstretched and hands clenched into fists.

But he senses him coming and at the last second the enemy ducks and Visionary knocks out the Terror. Stunned by this sudden change in battle Visionary is surprised and knocked out by another enemy.

Accelerate and Sea King have been caught by the one they have been fighting. He has them both by the throats and holding them in midair in each arm. Suddenly he drops them both to the floor and they fall like limp rags. He then holds his hand to his ears and bends over in pain. Then he falls down unconscious. From out of his ear comes the miniature might, the Atomic Sprite. He had played with their enemy's inner ear. It caused him so much pain he let go of Sea King and Accelerate before he could kill them. Then he passed out. Sprite didn't have much luck with his next victim. He was going to try the same thing, but he was ready for him. As Atomic Sprite tried to enter his ear he batted Sprite away from him. Sprite flew across the room. If not for the fact that he quickly grew back to normal height he would have been killed. He hit the wall and slid down to the floor as unconscious as the others.

Chapter 22

Invader From the Past

George Kirby has finally arrived at the building where our heroes are being held. It took him a little longer than the others. Not being a young man anymore he rarely gets out. Only recently had he dared to venture downtown to his meetings with Daniel. No longer having a driver's license he had to rely on public transportation to get here and even then he had to walk the last half a mile from the closest bus stop. But now that he was here what could he do?

"I know this was the last place they were, but I don't see them anywhere," he thinks to himself.

He tries the front door, but it is locked. He goes around to the back door but finds it too is locked.

When he tried to open the front door a warning light went off below. From a hidden camera, the Blue Hun and her men kept an eye on the elderly gentleman.

"He looks familiar to me, "said the Blue Hun.

She watched with interest. She hoped that he would just go away but saw he would not as he went around and approached the back door.

"Maybe he's just selling something," said one of her men.

"Open your eyes," said the Hun. "He's not carrying anything. Not even a clipboard to take a census."

Suddenly, as he walks away from the backdoor, George Kirby notices something in the yard. He goes over and tries to pick up a piece of black cloth. It seems to be stuck on something. He tugs with all his might till it finally pulls free. As he stares at it, he finally realizes what it is and his face lights up with recognition.

At the same time below the Blue Hun has ordered her man to get a close up of what George was looking at. Seeing his face light up made something click in her mind.

"I have seen that man before but he was much younger," she says. "He's looking at a piece of the Terror's cape. It must have caught on to our trap door when he fell. Now we have to take this old coot too. Open the door."

Her henchman complies with the order. He presses a button. Suddenly the ground beneath George opens up and swallows him whole. As he slides below to meet his captor the ground above is replaced and leaves no sign that he was ever there.

He lands with a thud at the end of his short journey. For a moment, George lies there as he takes time to assess his condition. Then he slowly rises to his feet. He winces in pain as his right arm seems to have broken from the fall.

"You took so long I feared that the fall may have killed you Mr. Kirby," says the Blue Hun from an intercom.

"Who are you? Where are my friends and how do you know my name?" He asks.

"All will be revealed to you soon," she replies.

A wall slides open. Instead of revealing a small army that it did moments ago to our other heroes it only shows two men this time. Both are in green suits, but no clip is seen on their belts and both are unarmed.

"Mr. Kirby please go with these men. They will give you a safe escort to me. Gentlemen please be gentle with him. He isn't a young man and by the way he is favoring that arm it may be broken."

As each man goes to his side George knows that he has no choice but to go with them willingly. The three of them walk toward the open end of the room. As they leave, the wall slides back into place. It leaves a huge empty room waiting for its next unwilling occupant.

Chapter 23

The Earth Dies Screaming

Moments later George is escorted into the control room where he sees a young woman wearing a blue jumpsuit. He still has no idea this is the new Blue Hun.

"Mr. Kirby, despite the circumstances, I must say it is an honor to meet the former Kid Patriot," she says.

"What makes you think I was Kid Patriot and where are my friends?" He asks.

"Don't insult me Mr. Kirby. I have seen old photos of Kid Patriot and his mentor Flag-waver. You may be older, but your facial features haven't changed that much. Other men your age wish they could say the same."

"Well, where are my friends? How could you have seen photos of me? That had to have happened decades before you were even thought of."

"Well, Mr. Kirby I happen to be a relative of an old combatant of yours. He had old photos and newspaper clippings with your picture in them. I never got to know him, but my Mother knew him very well. You see my Grandfather was the Blue Hun."

"You said was. Does that mean…"

"Yes Mr. Kirby he is dead and I hold you and Flag-waver responsible for the shame on my family."

"That's crazy Why are we responsible?"

"He may have died in the war but once it became known what his real name was it brought shame to my family that one of us was an enemy of the famous Flag-waver and Kid Patriot. Even his own family became ashamed of him. He never got a chance to defend himself and I never got to know my Grandfather."

George can only stare at this woman. He searches for words to say and finally he finds them.

"Does insanity skip a generation in your family?" He asks.

She takes a few steps closer to George. She raises her hand and slaps him with the back of her hand across the face.

"Do not call me insane. I have read my Grandfathers journals. He wanted only the best for Germany and the world. He was convinced that Hitler was the way."

"But Hitler himself was insane. All he wanted was power."

"Silence him!" She orders her men.

With the order given the two men on his sides tie his hands behind him and put a gag on his mouth.

"Over time I came to realize that Grandfather may be right. But I had no way of making it come about myself. Then, years ago, one night I was on my way home from work when I noticed something lying on the side of the road. I pulled over and picked it up. It was a belt. It was unique looking and there was no identification as to whom it belonged. I didn't intend to keep it at first but somehow I knew I had seen this belt before. I quickly went home and checked my Grandfathers old photos. Flag-waver was wearing the belt. I decided then and there that I had to see if this was his source of power. I discovered it was, but it wouldn't work on me. The belt itself wouldn't work for anyone else so it must have been made to work only for Flag-waver."

She walks over to a table. There she picks up a clip that we have seen the men that our heroes have fought.

"I have used the belt as a model," she says. "I have miniaturized parts of the belt to clip onto the belts of other men. For some, it gives them more stamina others more strength. Other men can't handle the power and die."

She goes over to the control panel and presses a button. In a corner of the room, a square hole opens in the floor. From that hole up comes a platform. On top of that platform, in a glass case, is Flag-wavers belt.

"There it is Mr. Kirby, Flag-waver's belt. A weapon that helped save the world from Germany. But now in the 21st century will now help me gather a mighty army to take it over. SO NOW IS THE TIME AND THE NEW BLUE HUN WINS!"

She presses another button on the control panel. Suddenly, part of the wall behind the panel slides back. From there George Kirby can see through a window into a testing area. He sees all his friends in harnesses as unwilling test subjects.

"Here are your friends Mr. Kirby. Now I am going to start a new phase in my research. To see what will happen if we try it on those that already have superpowers."

She then turns and walks out of the room. George knows that he has to find a way to get out of this. He has to find a way to free his friends. But how can he? His mouth is gagged so he can't yell and his hands are bound so he can't untie the gag or attack the two men watching him.

As he looks into the room where his friends are being held he sees the Blue Hun as she enters the room. She gives an order and two of her technicians apply a capsule to the side of each of the heroes. All that is except for Mr. Stretchable as he already has one on his side. From his point of view, they all seem to be holding up well with the exception of Brown Bolo. George can tell from her face that she is in extreme pain. That look on her face reaches George and he decides to take action. George launches his whole body into one of his guards and it causes a domino effect as he falls onto the other guard. The last guard hit his head on the side of the control panel and is knocked unconscious. Before the other guard can gather his senses and get to his feet, George kicks over the glass case that contains Flag-wavers belt. It crashes to the floor and breaks open.

The other guard is now starting to get up. George has an idea but doesn't know for certain it will work. Still it is the only idea he has and he has to act quickly. He steps behind the belt that is now lying on the floor. He plans to bend down and try to get it with his hands that are still tied up. But then something unexpected happens. The belt seems to fly up off the floor and around George's waist where it then fastens itself.

The guard is now on his feet and he takes a step toward George. Suddenly he is blinded by a flash of light. When the light fades the guard opens his eyes to see the star spangled garbed figure of the Flag-waver in the place of George Kirby. He is still bound and gagged. Still sensing that there is a danger, George reacts instinctively and breaks his bonds with his new found super strength. He takes off his gag then picks up the guard and throws him out of the room.

George is stunned at what he has just done. He is trying to figure out what happened when he catches a glimpse of himself in a reflective portion of the control board.

"Oh my gosh! I look like I did when I was 25. Why am I wearing Flag-waver's uniform? The only difference is that for some reason I have a cape."

While he is still trying to figure it out he looks again into the adjoining room. He sees again the experiments taking place and the pained expression on the Brown Bolo and is reminded why he is there.

With his new found power, George decides to

take matters into his own hands once again. He then jumps through the window into the laboratory.

The Hun and her men are startled as a new mask hero comes crashing into the room. Shards of glass glisten as they fall to the floor.

"Who are you?" Ask the Blue Hun.

"If you're the new Blue Hun then I'm the new Flag-waver," he says.

"That voice! It's Kirby! The belt works for him. Get him we need to study him," she orders her technicians. They attack him, but the new Flag-waver quickly disposes of them. Then he makes his way to the Brown Bolo. He grabs the capsule on her side and gets it off of her. She is still locked in the harness, but the expression of pain slowly fades from her face.

Just then the Blue Hun, seeing her plans quickly going up in smoke releases Mr. Stretchable from his harness.

"You think you have won! Well, I have had him in my power long enough bring him around to the right side. He is now a defender of the Blue Hun."

Suddenly Mr. Stretchable turns his hands into sledgehammers and tries to pound the new Flag-waver to death. Thankfully one of George's new powers is quickened reflexes and he is able to avoid them. Meanwhile, the other men of the Blue Hun's enter the room. No matter how quick he is he can't avoid them all. Eventually, he is surrounded and Mr. Stretchable gets him in his grip. He can tell that the capsule has increased his strength and he is crushing the life out of him. Mr. Stretchable has his arms bound to his side. He tries to break free, but their strength is too evenly matched. Mr. Stretchable pulls Flag-waver in closer and when he is close enough, Flag-waver kicks the capsule off of Mr. Stretchable but it seems to have little effect.

"Maybe they've all been under her spell too long," he thinks.

While their new found strength is evenly matched Flag-waver knows the continued struggle is his only chance to stay alive. The other men now close in on him seeing that he is holding his own against Mr. Stretchable. They start pounding on him till Flag-waver starts to pass out from the pain. He fights off the pain and suddenly shouts.

"Enough!"

Mr. Stretchable still holds him in his grip but stops squeezing. The other men stop hitting him and they just stand there and look at him.

"Can't you all see you've been taken in? That woman has control of you through the use of those capsules. If she takes over she will become America's dictator, not its savior. America is a great and beautiful pearl, but it is nothing without an ideal of freedom that is committed to making all men and women free. The reason I fought Hitler was because I knew that freedom is fragile. We can't let anyone snuff out the flame of freedom. It isn't free. Freedom is paid for with the blood and sweat of all our soldiers. Our country is being beaten down just like you were trying to do to me. People like the Blue Hun have almost beaten our country down to nothing. But it isn't there yet. It is still possible to bring America back to the ideals that formed the foundation that this country was built upon."

Somehow his words reach deep into the hearts of these men. Slowly they each reach for the capsule clipped to their side and remove them. Mr. Stretchable releases his grip on Flag-waver.

"No! It can't end this way!" Shouts the Blue Hun.

She runs back to the control room. Flag-waver goes after her.

"You're trapped Hun," says Flag-waver.

"There is still a way out," she replies.

"How? I'm standing between you and the door. The only other way is through that hole in the window in the lab. But Mr. Stretchable is in there releasing the others and they will stop you."

"A good leader plans for everything," says the Blue Hun.

She sits down in a chair next to the control panel. She presses a button and a glass tube encircles the chair.

"You only have a few moments Mr. Kirby. I pressed a self-destruct button. This lab and the building above will come crashing down very soon."

After that, the seated Blue Hun is ejected to the

top of the tube to the outside world. Flag-waver quickly jumps through the hole in the window and approaches Mr. Stretchable.

"We have to get everyone out of here! This place is gonna blow up!"

With all the heroes released Mr. Stretchable makes one of the technicians show them a way out. The only way that he knows is a long underground staircase that leads to the building above.

"Are you sure this is the only way out?" Ask Mr. Stretchable.

"It's the only way I know. I've never entered or left by any other way."

So they all get up the stairs as fast as they can. Venusian Visionary and the Golden Guardian both grab two men each and fly them up the stairs. Just as they enter the upper building they hear a rumbling underground. Then as the last one leaves the building it starts to crumble from the inside out.

Chapter 24

Mr. Stretchable's Moment of Truth

Later the next day Daniel has George Kirby and Mr. Stretchable over for dinner. After they eat they go to Daniel's den to discuss the previous day's adventure.

"Well, we proved that we worked pretty well as a group yesterday," says Daniel.

"That we did," says George.

"The reason why I only wanted to see you two tonight is because out of everyone you are the two who this adventure changed the most. What are you going to do now George?" Ask Daniel.

"I don't know. I was collecting my pension but can I now that I'm 25 again?" Replies George.

"I can always find a place for you at the Urich Foundation. What about you Stretchable? I've been paying you straight cash because you didn't know if you could trust me. Has this adventure proven my trustworthiness?"

"It has but I still can't tell you my name," replies Mr. Stretchable.

Daniel is deeply disappointed. He thought that this would be the breakthrough that he needed to gain Stretchable's trust.

"Why can't you tell me?"

"Well, this is embarrassing but I guess I can tell you two."

Stretchable paces back and forth in the room. George and Daniel are quiet as they can see that he is searching for the right words to say. Finally, he stops in the middle of the room. He looks Daniel right in the eye and tells him why he won't tell him his name.

"I can't remember my real name."

"You mean you got amnesia after some fight?" Ask George.

"I don't know how I got it. All I know is that one day I woke up and I had this strange power. Well, now I have two after this adventure."

"You still have that super strength from yesterday?" Ask Daniel.

"Yeah, I pulled the door off the taxi that brought me to work this morning."

"What's the name on your lease or mortgage?"

"I don't know where I live. I woke up in the middle of the street. So that is where I live. On the streets."

"We can't have that. You can stay with me," says George.

"Are you sure?" Ask Stretchable.

"You can help me understand what it's like to be young in this century and I can help you find out who you really are."

"Well, I see that you two are getting along fine. Gentlemen I think this group is off to a fine start."

With that George and Stretchable get ready to leave. George looks at Stretchable.

"You might as well see your new home tonight."

"I guess. I don't have to pack. All I have are the clothes on my back."

With that, Daniel walks them to the door. They look outside and see Daniel's limo and driver standing there with the passenger side door open.

"Where's the cab that brought us?" Questioned Stretchable.

"I called and cancelled the cab. I thought I would save you some money and have Louis drive you home," says Daniel.

On that note, they say their goodbyes. As they get in the car George tells Louis his address. Soon they are driving down the street heading for a new home for one and the promise of a new adventure for them both.

Get this book to see how Amazing
Fantasy #15 influenced people from
1962 to today.

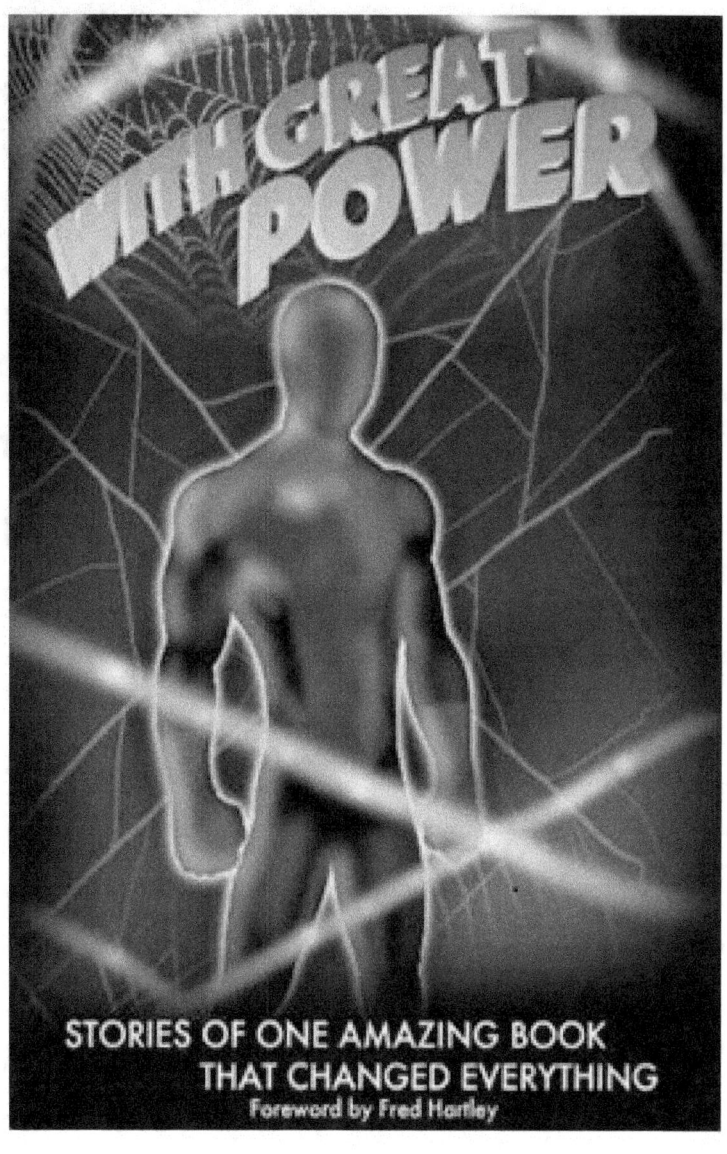

The Project: Hero saga continues in
Project: Hero Atlantis Under Attack.
On sale now from Dinky Publishing.

Also from Dinky Publishing is the book that started it all. A great Christmas story for the kids. Dinky the Elf!

Monkee fans rejoice! You can follow the further adventures of Davy Jones and the Monkees in Last Train to Murder and Other Stories. Mystery, action and adventure with a twist of the Monkees humor.

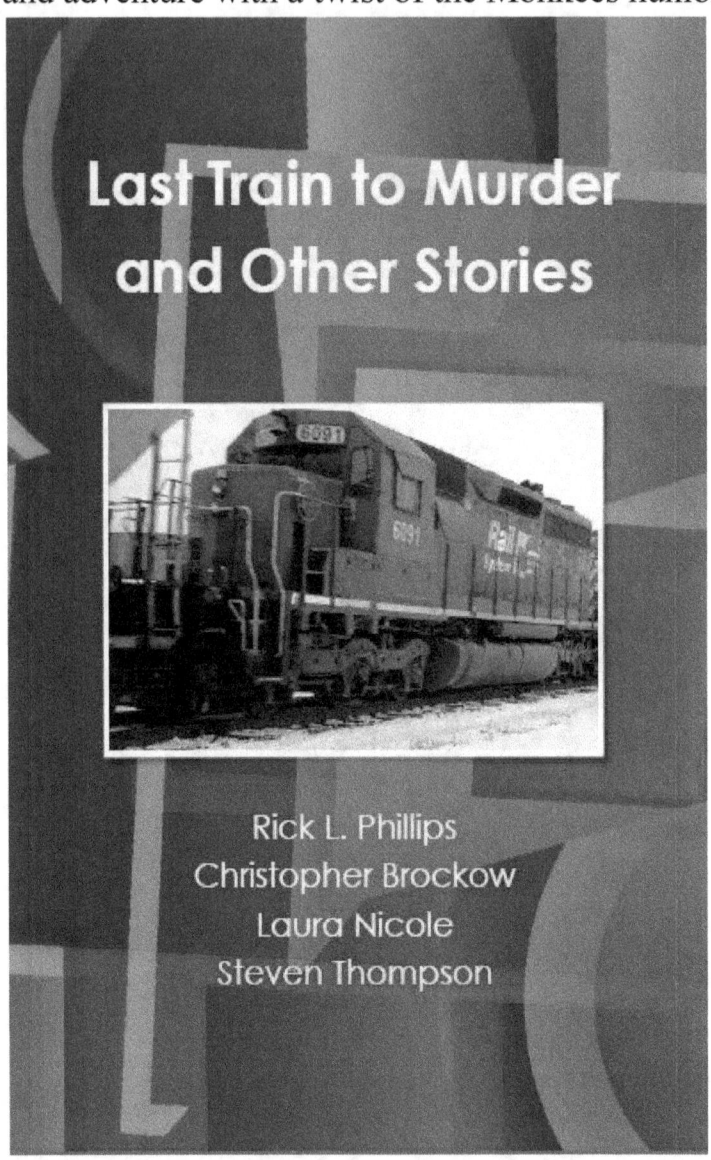

Last Train to Murder and Other Stories

Rick L. Phillips
Christopher Brockow
Laura Nicole
Steven Thompson

ABOUT THE AUTHOR

Rick L. Phillips was born in Covington, Ky to Louis and Margaret Phillips. He received a BA in Radio, Television and Film Production from Northern Kentucky University. He is an announcer and voice actor and his agent is the Heyman Talent Agency in Ohio, Kentucky and Indiana. His first professional story was a short story titled "War Between Two Worlds" published in the book "It's That Time Again Volume 3". It was edited by the late, great writer and editor Jim Harmon. His next book was a children's story called "Dinky the Elf". Later he penned the lighthearted murder mystery "Last Train to Murder".

He is a Christian and taught Sunday School for three years at his home church, Elsmere Baptist, where his Father was a Deacon and both parents were Sunday School Teachers there as well. He has sang in the choir for years and has directed choirs, sang solos and was part of a vocal gospel group called "Jubilation". Later he moved his membership to Erlanger Baptist where he serves as a Deacon and is a member of their choir and praise team and helps with the Lord's Supper.

www.ingramcontent.com/pod-product-compliance
Lightning Source LLC
Chambersburg PA
CBHW061214170626
46809CB00003B/1347